# The Vanishing on Maple Street

Lila Graves

# Contents

# Chapter 1

----------------------------------------------------------------

We all know and can agree easily that the first day of school is probably the most awkward, weirdest and tense days in history and it just repeats itself every year. I think that is a clear and agreeable statement. But do you know what's even worse than that? I can tell you right now: your first day of school in freshman year of high school, starting in November. That's right! My first day of school is tomorrow and I can't even begin to tell you or unravel my nerves about how scared I am.          There's truly no reason to be—it'll be the same people from middle school, I still have my group of friends that I love and I am definitely going to try out for cheer for the winter season. But still. I'm going to show up and everyone will be like "Ehmagawd where have ya been?!" "OMG did you hear that Baby Gantz is back!" or "Wow, Zayne's sister got fat..." but whatever. I know that this just has to be done.

I'm not some sort of drop out, by the way. Nothing like that. It's just last year, when I was in eighth grade, I was signed onto a modeling contract in Australia. So my mom let me leave school (I was home schooled for ten months) and we had to go to Australia so I could pursue this opportunity! Which, by the way, was absolutely incredible. The agency had contacted me last October, which is now a year ago, and I had the most amazing time. The contract was supposed to last only for three months, but after I finished their Summer catalogue I was picked up by a company in New York which sent me to London for six months. Let me tell you, London was absolutely incredible. I loved every second of it. After London, my contract had expired so they wanted to renew it but I was offered to do a commercial for a clothing line in California, so I chose that instead. I spent a month in California and ended up doing three different commercials: one for clothing, one for perfume and another for jewelry. It was an amazing experience. During that month I was offered to go to Paris for a runway show, so of course I hopped on that opportunity and I have just spent the last three months, since August, in Paris. I know, I know, I'm lucky. It's been such an incredible year. I did a lot of work in Paris: four runway shows, nine magazine COVERS, three Parisian commercials and I was a brand representative for a huge clothing department there—they sent me to Greece for a week when they branched out their new shop. Truly beautiful.

During this whole run around the globe, my mom came with me. She had to. She wasn't about to let her then-fourteen year old daughter go across the world on her own. So she came with me, and to be frank, I was glad. I was really nervous and scared since I hadn't really modeled before and I knew I was pretty—skinny, high cheek bones, long legs—that kind of anorexic, skinny-girl model type. I was always insecure about my body since I wanted to be like my older sister, Kim. Kim had curves and huge boobs and abs and a big ass and all the guys loved her in high school. That's what I wanted. I wasn't anorexic, I actually ate a lot, but I never gain weight and I can't just force my body type. I'm grateful for what I have though. I developed some more, actually have boobs and my butt is starting to shape. I'm grateful.

My dad had to stay home since he is a partner at a law firm. He was really proud of me though and was grateful that he had my mom to come along with me. He came and visited us in Australia for two weeks with my brother, Zayne. They spent Christmas and New Years with us last year in Australia. When we were in England, my mom flew to the Caribbean for Valentine's day and spent the weekend there with my dad. I was left alone, but at that point I already had a personal assistant who was around my mom's age so that's who was left to "take care" of me. The only time I was able to go back to North Carolina was in April, when Easter came. I was happy to fly back home for the weekend and spend it with my family—my siblings all missed me dearly, I was able to see two of my best friends and then I had to go back to England. In July, when I was in California, one of my best friends flew over to see me (since my mom paid for her ticket). Kylie and I had an amazing time together for that week. She came with me to all my shoots and my hairdresser and makeup artist loved her and she loved them. We had a fabulous time and I wish she could've stayed longer. I always Skyped with my girls, my sister Kim and my dad. I love them all to death and couldn't have asked for better support.         The past few months we've been in Paris, so my dad came for a week and a half with my sister, her boyfriend, my older brother Keith, his girlfriend Penny, Pappy, and my best friend Kylie. We all had a really good time while they were here and my mom didn't even ask any questions when Kylie and I were coming home with my siblings at seven am the next day. It was so much fun!

My dad picked my mom and I up from the airport Monday morning and now it's Wednesday. I didn't really want to leave—I've made tons of friends from all over the place and I miss them so, so much. Of course we're all friends on Facebook now and they follow my Instagram. But still. We had so many late nights' together and early mornings and I will miss all of them with all my heart and I hope that they'll find the time to come visit me this year. I honestly do love modelling—it's not that I don't. I would've signed on again to be in Paris or I got a few other offers—a company in Japan, a runway show in Italy or a swimsuit catalogue in Hawaii. I wanted to go, I did, but I just felt so burnt out from Paris. It's so hard to constantly be working while trying to maintain schoolwork. It's so hard to be away from my dad and my family and friends. I miss them. And not only that, but I feel bad for my mom. She had to give up so much time away from her other kids and from my dad and from her own mom so I felt a bit guilty. I know she loves me no matter what and supported me 1000% on whatever I wanted to do. So I figure why not go back to North Carolina, and maybe I'll fly out on some weekends to do small projects rather than be away from everyone for months at a time.      When my dad picked us up from the airport on Monday he was probably the happiest guy to ever live. He was so grateful that we were home safe and sound and that he had his wife back. I think my mom was pretty happy too, she was probably homesick although she never said a word to me about it.

# Chapter 2

After we loaded our suitcases (seven of them) into the family van, I was so happy to be back home and to go back to my street and to see all my friends. We stopped at a diner just a town over because my mom was extremely hungry and hates airplane food. I didn't really eat because I was so excited to go home and to see my brothers and sister. This weekend we are going to have a Welcome-home party for me. I'm excited about that. My parents really are the best.

After the diner my parents and I got back in the van and it really felt like an eternity before we reached my house—I nearly bawled when I got home to see balloons and my three best friends—Melanie, Laura and Kylie all waiting outside on my porch for me. They all skipped school so that they could see me!

We spent Monday relaxing. They helped me unpack my stuff and they encouraged me to tell them some of my stories, which I didn't even know where to begin because of so many crazy nights. At around seven o'clock that night my sister Kim came home from work and then Lucas came over—her boyfriend—and I was so happy to see them! They're honestly my favorite couple and we always have a good time together. Melanie and Laura had to go home for supper at around that time and Kylie stayed over to eat dinner with us. Later that night Keith came home and greeted me and had gotten me a special gift, which ended up being tickets to a basketball game in Charlotte. I'm kind of excited about that, since it will be Keith, Kim, Lucas, Zayne and I going to see the game.

Yesterday I went to the mall with my mom and we shopped for clothes, she let me get a blow-out for school and we got our nails done together. We picked up Kylie from school at three o'clock and we all went and saw a movie together. Then last night I joined Kylie at her yoga class that she goes to (I didn't know she started yoga!) and we all went home and she slept over. So this morning Kylie went to school and I stayed home another day because I was too tired and didn't feel like seeing everyone from school. My mom told me that I am going tomorrow no matter what my excuse is of not going, and I told her fine and agreed to it. I might as well. It's almost six o'clock at night now, and—"Em!?" I hear a shout from downstairs. I get up, placing my journal on the bed and run over to the balcony that overlooks my living room."What?" I ask softly. Why are they yelling?"Let's go to The Teacup." I groan. I don't want to go to The Teacup but Kim wants me to... so I guess I will."Fine." I run back into my room and grab a cardigan. It's still warm outside, but sometimes at night it gets a bit chilly.I walk downstairs and loop my arm through Kim's, and we leave.

"I can't even believe you're going to be a freshman in high school," Kim says to me. I roll my eyes."I'm already a freshman, I just need to go to school," I correct her. She laughs."Right, right. I remember my high school years. Let me tell you this much baby girl: don't waste a single moment. High school is the fucking bomb. Drink a lot but to the point where you're still walking and you'll be fine," now it's my turn to laugh."Let's not forget England, or Paris for that matter..." She starts to giggle, thinking of the memory. Probably the same night that I'm thinking about right now as well."If we're going to talk about Paris then I want to know if you're still with Peter. I didn't want to ask you as soon as you got back, but now that you've had..."

"We're still together," I say through tight lips. I don't want to talk about it. "Oh okay." Is all she says. She doesn't want to talk about it either. So if she doesn't want to talk about it, why bring him up at all? She changes the subject."Are you excited to see Pat tomorrow?" How could she even mention him!? Of course I'm not excited. He's probably the last person I want to see."No." I answer flatly. Kim is such a bitch."Why?" She sounds earnest, as if she doesn't know."Because I have a boyfriend. And because why would I be excited to see him? He barely tried to talk to me this past year and he messed with me so much before I left. He's a player," I don't want to sound angry about him; I want to sound indifferent. I don't really care for him. I don't."Ah, okay. I don't know. I heard from people that he missed you and he's really looking forward to seeing you." "That's nice." I'm not going to give her, or anyone, satisfaction of a reaction.

We park the car and I get out, strolling casually into The Teacup. And of course the first people I have to see are the people I hate the absolute most. Lindsay, Caitlyn and Marnie all stare at me, in shock. As if they've seen a ghost. I raise an eyebrow, this five-second stare down now over, and they all run up to me in excitement."Seriously?! Is this even real? Is this a joke? Where have you been!?" Caitlyn squeals. I don't actually hate Caitlyn, I just hate that she's friends with these other two bitches. They've always hated me—especially Lindsay. Because Lindsay's always been so in love with Pat. "I um... I got back Monday," I tell them. Caitlyn hugs me and I put my arms around her gently, cautiously."Are you coming to school again?" Marnie asks me. She seems indifferent about me, and I nod my head yes."I'm going back tomorrow," I tell them."Yay! What hour do you have lunch?""Eleven o'clock,""Perfect! You can sit with us tomorrow, if you want," Caitlyn says excitedly. Lindsay is giving her the nastiest glare. Suddenly, she turns to me and says:"Oh, that'd be good. You can tell us all about your adventures," She says with a smile that reminds me of how a predator feels when it's about to eat their prey. I nod, "yeah definitely" I say flatly before returning to my sister. My sister looks at me with a smirk."Friendly girls, huh," she sounds so sarcastic. I nod."Don't even get me started... of course we have to run into them of all people. So annoying. Take me back to Paris." My sister laughs and we order our coffees and croissants.

# Chapter 3

When we return home, Kim goes into the garage because Keith's in there with his band and I walk around to the front of our house to go inside. And, cursed by Satan himself, who is standing outside on my front porch? Pat.

"Wow," is all he says as I approach him. I have butterflies in my stomach—or maybe I'm in knots, but I lose my voice for a second looking at him. I open my mouth to say something but nothing comes out. He pulls me in for a hug and in those couple of seconds I feel good, I feel safe, I feel better and I want to stay like that. He pulls away and looks at me.

"You're gorgeous." I snort. As if I haven't heard that before. "Thanks.""Let's catch up," Pat says. I raise an eyebrow."Here?" He shakes his head, then points to a car two houses over."You have a car?" "You bet I do." He takes the keys from his pocket, jingling them, and I soon find myself in the passenger seat of his car, parked in an empty parking lot a town over. "SO, old friend, how has your year been?"

I shrug my shoulders."Fantastic. And you?" I try to sound casual, as if I don't have a bunch of stories I'm ready to spill. As if I don't have a boyfriend I'm completely, hopelessly in love with."It was alright. I'm glad to be a junior in high school. I'm glad to have a car. I'm glad that football season is almost over. You really have changed," I try to smile but I don't know what he means. Is that good or bad?"Uh, thanks. So have you. You look good," I'm being completely genuine with him. He looks more than good; he looks so hot. "Thanks, babe. You didn't really get back to me with the Facebook messages I sent you..." he says, trying to get me to say something back. I look down."Yeah, sorry. I know. I was busy. And you were... far. I don't know. I just didn't think it was important and plus, I mean, now... you're in a relationship, aren't you? With Shannon?" Don't even get me freaking started about freaking Shannon. She's probably one of the biggest whores in South Hamelton Hills and she has fucked more guys then I can count on eight hands. I know all about it, because Kylie has kept me in the loop and been a good little spy on Pat.

"I mean, yeah. Nothing serious though.""Facebook official," I remind him. He rolls his eyes. And of course, his phone rings, and who is it? Shannon."You know you still want me," he says to me in a soft tone. I laugh. Out loud. "No, I don't," I say dryly. "Yeah, you do. I see it in your eyes," He bites his lip. Oh, he's so... not Peter. "It wouldn't matter if I did. I have a boyfriend, Pat." His face turns to ice. He looks blankly at me, but I could've sworn I saw a flash of despair."Re—really?" he stammers. He's trying to keep his cool."Yeah. And he's wonderful," I say happily. Pat nods. "How'd you meet? What's his name?""His name's Peter. He's amazing, I met him in England and like... I don't know, he's perfect. He's eighteen." I smile happily and Pat gives a rough laugh."So he lives in England...and you live here. How will that work?" He asks skeptically. I shrug."I don't know, he's coming for Christmas, to stay. He doesn't live in England though. He lives in New York." Pat nods."Right, of course he does. And you like him?" "Of course I do! I love him." Yes—I definitely saw it. Pat's face is indifferent, but his eyes say it all; they look like they could have tears in them. I don't care though. He has Shannon after all, right?

"You... you love him?" I think he's going to explode; he can't hold it in much longer. "Yeah! He's honestly the best thing that could've ever walked into my life. I'm so grateful to have him be mine. And I'm all his." I smile dreamily out the car window, while Pat's eyes bore a hole into the side of my face because he's staring at me so hard. I keep my eyes focused on the clouds passing in the sky. "That's...I'm happy for you. You do deserve to be loved by someone, as long as he treats you well. Or else I'll kick his ass," he says gruffly. "Nah, you don't have anything to do with it. I have brothers for that," I tell him. Pat looks so riled up though and I can tell he's hurt, and I can tell that I'm pushing buttons. And I love it. That's exactly what he deserves.

# Chapter 4

**P**AT

    She said it staring right at me. She loves him. She loves this kid. Her... her boyfriend. Oh, please, Em, shut the fuck up! You don't love him! How could you LOVE him!? OVER ME?! We're childhood sweethearts for crying out loud and right now you're spurring out shit like you have exploding diarrhea or something! YOU DON'T LOVE HIM!

    I wanted to scream that at her and slam my fist through the window but instead I sat there quietly, listening to her words, and trying to contain myself. I will not throw a fit, because I know that if I did she'll yell at me and never speak to me again and tell her boyfriend what an asshole I am. I want to look like the good guy here—hell, I am the good guy here! But for her to say it so straight faced, as if she actually believes she loves this kid, this New Yorker, who does she thinks she's kidding? Her dad would kill her if she dated one of those Yankees.

Her dad would kill her if she dated, period. But instead, I sat there. She started telling me how they met—at one of her shows in England, he came up to her after and told her she did really well and that she was beautiful. Of course, she is fucking beautiful, she doesn't need some dude to tell her that. Everyone knows it and so does she.

But then she tells me how he started taking her out, classy dinners, high-end bars, introducing her and networking her to many other people in the business, landing her a few deals in California and some shows in Paris. Fucking ridiculous. She tells me he's absolutely exquisite, Pat, and that I'll love him. Trust me, I won't love any guy you ever talk to, ever. That's what I want to tell her. I don't. Instead, I sit there with my mouth fucking shut because if I open it I know I won't shut up and I'll say something that will upset her.

Oh, and you know what else, Pat? We went on little weekend trip up to some random bed and breakfast spots in the countryside of England, which were absolutely magnificent. So beautiful. You would've loved it, she adds. Why is she doing this to me? She knows she's hurting me; I KNOW that she knows she's hurting me but instead she keeps on ranting her mouth, that beautiful jaw, those beautiful lips, her beautiful smile. At least he makes her happy. Thing is, I want to be the one to make her happy.

# Chapter 5



P AT

As she continues to blabber on about how great Prince Peter is, I sort of try to zone myself out to the night before she left, back to last October. The night before she took off for her flight to New York to transfer to LA to go to Australia. She was with all her girlfriends that night at the lake. Some of the kids from the street were there, Zayne was there with some of the boys, so I had joined them. I hadn't realized she was leaving so soon. But she was. And I got scared shitless. I was terrified. I wanted her to stay a little bit longer, we were doing so well... but I knew she couldn't, and I was afraid of her leaving. I had so many feelings for her and I was afraid if she left that she would never know how I felt, and I knew that she felt the same. I took her hand that night and we walked through the trail near the lake, by ourselves. She was a little tipsy and I was completely sober, and we laughed as we walked and I told her I'd really miss her and she said that she'd miss me. And I looked at her and I knew I had to kiss her, and I did, against a tree and I held her there and she kissed me back and gave me a rueful smile afterward and it made my heart... my heart flutter. I wanted her.

And I told her to not forget about me and I told her to make me proud. I told her I'll be waiting for her when she got back and goddamit I waited—I saw that she'd read my texts and I knew she wasn't answering me and I knew something was wrong. And in the summer when Kylie went to see her I gave Kylie a bracelet and a letter to give to her, to Emma. And goddammit I waited for her! I did! We would constantly be messaging each other initially, but soon her messages got shorter until they became nonexistent. I missed her. I needed her. I realized that. I was completely infatuated by a girl who could care less. And it hurt. And it still fucking hurts. I waited until Kylie returned from California to realize whatever Emma and I had was over, even if it never began. And so I went back to partying, I went back to drinking and getting high and going to raves and eventually started hooking up exclusively with Shannon until Shannon said she wouldn't have sex with me anymore unless we were together-together and she was my actual titled girlfriend. So I agreed. Whatever. It's not liked the love my life is across the Atlantic anyway.

One day when I was scrolling through my Facebook feed there was such a promiscuous picture of Emma that she had been tagged in. Her long, tan body was draped over a guy's shoulder, and her mascara was running but she must've been laughing because she had a huge, loopy smile on her face, and one of her legs was kicked up in the air and she was barefoot and her arms were flailing and she had her heels in her hands and she was wearing extremely short shorts and a crop top that showed her clearly visible belly ring and beautiful body. Her hair was so long and it looked so gorgeous, even after whatever sort of night she had, had. She must've been in England at that time and I was so jealous and upset that she was with another guy. Of course, I never told her. But she looked beautiful. Anyway, a few days later when I tried to retrieve the picture so I could ask one of my friends what he thought of it, it was gone. She must have untagged herself or something because I couldn't find it anywhere and I secretly feel like she just wanted me to see it so I could be suspicious or know that that was her way of saying she was over me.

# Chapter 6

P<sup>AT</sup>

"Pat?" she asks me, she's finally stopped staring out the window and is back to looking at me. I hope she doesn't realize how I feel."Yeah?" She pauses."How are you and Shannon?" She doesn't even seem to mind; she asks so casually. As if it's normal for us to go our separate ways and pretend that nothing ever happened.

"We... we're fine. I don't think it's as serious as yours sounds to be, that's for damn sure," I manage to laugh. She nods. She knows I'm a player. Of course, I'm not serious. She knows I'm a slut. Of course, I'm not serious about a girl. "Ah, that's okay. One day you'll be serious with someone," With you, I almost say. But I don't. I can't. I don't want her to be scared off. Once again, I rather shut the fuck up and scream about it later then give her a clue about what's going on in my mind.

"Anyway, I should probably get home. We have school in the morning." School. Right. Shit."When do you have lunch?" "Sixth. And you?""Same. Sit with me tomorrow." She starts to laugh, more like a cackle. I look at her like she's crazy. "You know who told me to sit them with tomorrow?" "Who?""Lindsay." I start to laugh too. I remember how much Em hated Lindsay, and how much Lindsay hated her. Rumor has it, it was because of a special someone...

"Well tell Lindsay to go fuck herself and that you're going to come and sit with me tomorrow. I'll buy you lunch," I wink. Emma groans. She hates when I act like this, cocky."Maybe. I have other fans, ya know." I nod. That's true. Everyone at school thinks she's like a celebrity. Relax yourselves. She's mine.

She was, at least.

# Chapter 7

P <sup>AT</sup>

I take Emma home and go home myself. We only live a few houses apart. Next door neighbors all the way. When I park my car I see that Terrence still isn't home. He lives across the street from me and he's one of my good friends. I walk in the house to smell my mom's cooking and my dad's sitting at the table reading an article at the table. "Hey! So get your siblings? Devyn's with Brynn and I think Wyatt and Shawn are riding bikes outside—but Mrs. Fritt is outside watching them. Just let them know dinner's ready," I nod. The joy of having a big family.

"Wait—is Kelly coming?" Kelly's my lovely older sister. When we were younger I used to fight constantly with her but we got over that stage real quick. I trust her with all my heart and I love her to death. I see my mother shift uncomfortably, looking away from me and turning back to the meal she's preparing. I take that as a no.

I don't know why, since nobody really wants to speak about it but for some reason there's been a drift in the household between my parents and Kell. I don't know what she did or if she did anything at all for that matter, but Kelly's barely been showing up to the house. As I walk outside, I take out my phone and call her."Hello?" She basically screams into my ear."Hey! Kell, ouch. What's going on? You coming for dinner?" Silence. "I—I wasn't asked to come," I don't say a word. I don't know why she wasn't asked to come."Oh, mom probably forgot. Come for dinner. I don't want to be with the youngins' by myself," I hear grunting."Listen, I'll call you back. Maybe catch up this week. I gotta go," I hear someone yell her name and she abruptly hangs up. What the hell was that all about?

I pass by the Colowski's house, where Devyn, my twelve-year-old sister is hanging about at. They're in the back-yard dancing to some pop music."We gotta go eat dinner," I say as I approach. I see Harry, Brynn's dad standing over his vegetable garden, picking tomatoes."Hey Mr. C!" He looks up and smiles at me. "Patrick! How're ya? Hold on, Candace has some veggies for yer mom. Let me go get her for yer," Hon-estly, these are the nicest people you'll probably ever meet. Harry and Candace Colowski absolutely adore my family so every time they see me they'll always give me loads of food or, usually, Devyn will come home with bags of food. I don't know why, but free food is free food. Mr. C hands me two bags filled with cucumbers, tomatoes and carrots. I say thanks and

Devyn and I walk away. I proceed across the street, a house over, where I see my brothers riding their bikes with a few of the other neighborhood kids. I don't know why they always come to Sylvia's house, Mrs. Fritt's, but they do. Apparently it's an extremely good area to ride bikes, as all the kids usually do. I smile at Mrs. Fritt's who is sitting on her porch, knitting. She's a quiet old lady and Kylie's great-aunt.

I tell my brothers to ride home, and Devyn and I walk back to my house."Guess what, Pat?" Devyn tells me as we're w alking."What?""Emma's back." I smile and pretend it's okay."I know. I saw her earlier. She looks great. You should stop by tomorrow after school and ask her if she's going to go back to being assistant coach for cheer for you guys," Her eyes brighten."That's a good idea! Yeah, I miss her. I can't wait to see her again! Is she really tan? Does she speak with an accent? She probably met so many hot boys." I sigh. I'm not having this conversation with my baby sister.

I get inside the house, my brothers are washing up, my mom's almost finished setting the table, my dad's already grabbing food and Devyn goes straight to the bathroom to clean up as well. I empty the bags from Mr. C into the fridge and grab a plate as well. We say grace and then dig in, even though my dad had already done that. Devyn starts telling us about school and how much she loves Brynn and they're best friends forever, meanwhile my little brothers are in the middle of spurting stories about how they are going on some field trip and are going to go hiking and asking my parents if they'll chaperone the trip. My dad gives it some consideration."I'll probably go with you guys," he tells them. I continue to eat, and then I look at my dad and ask him where Kelly is. He clears his throat.

"Guys, I guess we should speak about this now since Pat's brought it to attention. Your sister has decided to move out. She's still in Hamelton but renting a place with her... her boyfriend," my throat catches and I am about to burst into laughter or tears. "What?" I say. "Yeah, she's um. She'll be alright," my dad tells me. I look at my mother who is staring down at her plate. Did Kelly move out or was she kicked out? Does it make a difference, really? I try to breathe but my siblings act like it's not a big deal. My baby brother, Shawn says "It's not like we see her anyway." I kind of wanted to hit him but I know he's too young to understand.

# Chapter 8

-------------------------------------------------------

P AT

Dinner ends quickly and next thing I know it's fucking Thursday morning and I'm at the gym sweating my ass off and sore as hell. Terrence was supposed to meet me here but he's so lazy and didn't even show up or bother texting me that he wasn't going to come. I went on my own, since that's been the routine.

I shower in the gym locker room and then proceed to walk to my school locker. Shannon's at my side and I didn't even realize.

"Goodmorning baby," I kiss her on the lips. She smiles up at me. She's so innocent looking sometimes."Babe, we need to talk," she tells me. Her voice is silky smooth and sounds almost angelic. I nod my head, wishing for her to proceed. "Like, so...I know that we're pretty serious right now and all, so this weekend is my dad's wedding. Remember I told you he's remarrying? I want you to come to the wedding with me. I'd really, really appreciate it if you'd be my date...and I could introduce you to my family there." I want to vomit. I don't want to meet anyone in her family! "I—I don't know. I have a soccer tournament and..." She cuts me off."It's Saturday night. You just need to show up for the reception. Please, I love you." I close my eyes and try to think clearly, since I really don't want to meet any extended family—it was bad enough meeting her dad and his fiancée, accidentally, on a Saturday morning while I was trying to sneak my way out of the house.

I open my eyes three seconds later and look straight past Shannon to find Emma strutting down the hallway, looking flawless. Zayne, Kylie, Laura and Caitlyn are with her. I smile and then look back to Shannon.

"One second," I say to her. I close my locker and walk past her to Emma, who stopped to say hi to some group of girls. They're probably in her grade because I don't recognize them."Em," I say from behind her. She turns around and is startled to see me. She smiles. I pull her in to hug me and kiss her softly on her ear. I could feel her quiver in my arms. She liked it.

"Back off," Kylie says jokingly to me. I do, because I can feel Shannon's eyes boring into the back of my head and I don't want to start a fight with her—but I want everyone to know Emma and I talk. So every guy in this building can back the hell up from her. "What class do you have first?" I ask."English." The only boy in the group of girls she had approached high-fived her."English buddies!" he told her. I wanted to hit him."That's nice. Do you... do you want me to walk you?" Emma looked at Kylie, then back at me."Nah. I have to go catch up with some people. Nice seeing you though." Emma turned her back to me and went back to talking with the rest of the girls. I laughed and Zayne looked at me apologetically. "Don't," I said to him. I didn't want to hear a word."I didn't say anything man," he said back to me. I walk back to Shannon, who is giving me the dirtiest glare in the world. If looks could kill, I'd be dead.

# Chapter 9

I agreed to go to the wedding with Shannon. I felt bad. She's so manipulative. But eh. Whatever. It isn't like I'll be missing something else to go out and drink at an open bar with some hot chick who desperately loves having sex with me. That's the best part of Shannon to be honest—her legs are always open.

For me, at least.

Sixth period comes quickly and I go to the cafeteria to find Emma on line with some of the popular bitches that she was complaining about—Lindsay and Caitlyn. Shannon catches my eye and is sitting in our usual spot with my friends. I walk straight up to baby girl Emma, cutting the entire line—but who really gives a shit?—and put my arm around her shoulder. She looks up at me. She used her fingers to take my arm off her, as if I'm some sort of bug. "What?" I say to her. "Why are you here?" "You're sitting with me today." Emma gives the girls a look, as if OMG he's so annoying why the fuck is this loser talking to me? Meanwhile Lindsay and Marnie want my D. They'd love to be Em right now. "You don't need their permission to sit with my babe," I tell her. She turns a shade of red. Lindsay laughs."Fine. But then they have to sit with us too, okay?" She says evenly to me. A little awkward since the last time Lindsay and Shannon were within ten feet of each other, they nearly killed each other. Maybe Em knows this and is doing that on purpose. "Sounds good. See you soon buttercup," I walk away just as easily I came. I hope Em is embarrassed and is about to feel how much tension she's going to start up. But good for her—she wants to play a game, and she wants to play it her way. I'll go along with it. I don't care. As long as she ends up as mine, who gives a shit?

# Chapter 10

"I CANT BELIEVE WHAT JUST HAPPENED!" Seventh period—everyone is talking about it. Not only is the entirety of Hamelton Hills High School floating with gossip about Em, but now it's all about what happened sixth period. Fucking Em had to ruin it for all of us, since now both Shannon, Lindsay and Marnie all have detention together. After school. For the next four school days.

I don't know why they had to fight or why they were so compelled to, but next thing I know Shannon is cursing her out from across the table, calling her a whore and a bitch, and leaping over the table, tackling Lindsay to the floor. Obviously Lindsay's stupid and can't handle my girlfriend's wrath, so Marnie steps in and starts beating on my girlfriend as well. Em shrieks and grabs Lindsay off her, but winds up getting punched in the face by Marnie. She has a black eye.

Right now, in seventh period, I was able to go to class but Principal Locke took the girls—Shannon, Lindsay, Marnie and

Emma into her office. I felt bad for Em and I got really angry when Marnie punched her. I actually pulled Shannon from Lindsay and held her, putting my back to Lindsay so that she was hitting my back instead of Shannon. Shannon was trying to claw her way through my grip, but it wasn't happening. Enough was enough.

Now though the entire school is talking about it and is so fucking happy that Lindsay got a good beating. Even though Shannon probably would've lost, if Em hadn't done something to step in and distract Marnie from kicking her ass completely.

I'm sitting in my history class with two of my best friends—Jack and Terrence—and they are hysterical. They keep telling everyone in the class what happened and how it went down. They're so damn happy about it. They think it's funny. Like it's some big joke—oh my best friend's girlfriend got the shit beaten out of her.

I decide to text Em, to see how she's feeling. Hey. You ok?

She texts me back almost immediately: Your girlfriend's a bitch. She told Locke that it was me, Marnie and Lindsay...so I have detention with them as well. OF COURSE Lindsay and Marnie played along with it. SO THANKS.

Shit. I felt bad. Her first day of school and she gets detention. I'm almost positive everyone will be making fun of her and telling her why did she even bother coming back. That's something else I realized, a lot of the people in this school are so fucking jealous of Em it makes me sick to my stomach. I don't understand how you can be so hateful towards someone whose done absolutely nothing to you. But whatever. I have her back at least.

I'm sorry. Do you want me to try talking to Shan?

Why did I say Shan? She'll be like, nice fucking nickname for your whore, Pat.

No. And don't expect me to sit with you at lunch. Ever. I hate you, your girlfriend, and your fangirls. My mom's gonna kill me. Bye

Alright, she's taking it too far. Her mom won't kill her. She literally just got back. I need to talk Shan...hopefully she's in eighth period since that's the only class I have with her. I'm so disappointed that she'd rat out Em like that. But what do you expect? Jealousy gets the best of us. Or so they say.

# Chapter 11

I hate Pat, I hate Shannon, I hate Lindsay, I CAN'T STAND Marnie and I hate every single idiot who asked me if my black eye is from Marnie. Like who the heck do you think gave it to me?!

Honestly I shouldn't have stepped in. But my bad for trying to be nice and trying to pull Lindsay off Shannon, my bad. And Marnie going Hulk on me and fucking hitting me as hard as she could. I'm so upset. Peter's going to be so worried tonight when we Skype. I feel terrible. Not to mention, my mom will legitimately die if I tell her that I got detention. How come Keith can go through high school not once with a phone call home, let alone detention?! How come Zayne has never had the slightest bit of trouble in high school?! But oh, nooo... my daughters on the other hand are troublemakers! I don't want to be like Kim, I really don't. I wanted to have a good first day of high school. I really did. But I guess that won't be happening since I have to report to detention directly after ninth period.

Meanwhile all my teachers had asked me so far, "Is Kim your sister?" "Do you have a brother named Zayne?" "Don't tell me your Keith Grantz's sister!" Ha. Why yes I am. A loser in detention.

I come in late to seventh period where I see Kylie and Laura sitting in the back corner of my room. They saved me a seat. Thank God. I am so happy to have them as my protection. Immediately all eyes are on me: not only because I decided to come to school again after a year of missing it, but also because I got hit in the face and have a huge swollen black and blue eye. Way to be the center of attention. "I'm so sorry," Kylie says to me as I sit. I shake my head. It's fine. It's all fine. I grab my phone and pull up the texts from Pat, throwing it onto her desk, she looks at it and rolls her eyes. "You're so dramatic." I don't care. I have every right to be as dramatic as fuck. I want to tell my mom before anyone else tells her, but unfortunately I'm just stuck in class.

# Chapter 12

As soon as class ends I tell Kylie I need to meet Zayne to ask him what I should do. He tried calling me during class while he was at some internship meeting but I obviously couldn't pick up. I sprinted through the halls to Zayne as soon as the bell rang and met him in the lobby, running into his arms and I began to cry. Not cry, but wail. I couldn't help myself. I just felt so overwhelmed by my feelings and literally everyone in school was talking about me.

It was bad enough they would say things like "still anorexic?" or "It's disgusting how modeling companies take anorexic girls" or "she's not even that pretty, how did she ever model?" I'M NOT FUCKING ANOREXIC! I don't even look as bad as I used to—I gained weight! Why do they have to say anything at all? Shut up and be happy with your body! Please!

Kylie had followed me out of class and is standing near me as she waits for me to be done crying into my big brother's arms. I can see her eyes darting around the lobby; obviously everyone's staring at us and she's death-glaring them. "Don't worry, Emma. Mom won't be that mad... you were defending Shannon, right?""Yes! But still. Mom's going to be so pissed off. I hate him, Zayne. I hate him." I sound so angry, and I can tell I do by the way Zayne's eyes bug out and he looks at Kylie for help. Kylie rubs my back soothingly. I want to go home. I can't stand to be in this building a minute longer. I hear another person say something about me—"Oh she just got back and got into fight... attention whore, maybe?"

And next thing I know Kylie's pounced on this girl and started beating her fist into the girl's jaw. Why?! I grab Kylie by the arm trying to pull her off but she's strong and she refuses to budge. Why Kylie, why. Zayne pulls Kylie off and Kylie begins to cry as well."SAY ANOTHER WORD, BITCH. I FUCKING DARE YOU. SPEAK ABOUT HER AGAIN AND I SWEAR, I'LL FUCKING KILL YOU!!!!!!!!" Kylie's screeching this at the poor girl who's trying to pick up her books from the ground.

I'm so grateful to have Kylie as a friend. "Ky, calm down," Zayne whispers in her ear. "Fuck off," I say to the crowd that's developed around us. This is what we do; draw attention. Principal Locke pushes her way through the crowd and stands before us.

"Again," She sounds defeated. "To my office," The girl with the bloody nose, Kylie, Zayne and I all report to her office. I feel so terrible. I need to go home. My mom's going to be pissed that Zayne is involved in this as well. My phone buzzes as I am following Principal Locke, second time today, to her office. What the hell happened?!

Pat. Fuck him.

I shove my phone into my messenger bag and keep my eyes low as we enter her office. The Vice Principal, Dethla, is there. I sink into the seat. "Why are we here again?" Principal Locke is handing the bloody-nosed girl a tissue box.

"Because of this bitch over here," Kylie's still huffing and puffing as she speaks. She needs to relax or she's going to get into more trouble. Principal Locke raises her eyebrows. "Not in my office. Zayne, explain the story please." Principal Locke is extremely fond of my brother; he's going to be Valedictorian of the senior class after-all. "Well...my sister was crying and upset and I was comforting her, with Kylie. Then this girl over here said something about my sister and Kylie defended her." He spoke rather objectively; that was the truth. "Uh-huh. And you know, we have freedom of speech." "Do you understand what it's like to be a best friend, Principal Locke? This is my BFF's first day of school after a year away. Kids are hating on her for being successful already and all making their own judgments. She tried to break up a fight between an upperclassman and a lower classman and got shitted on. She has a black eye because of a stupid bitch and she has detention because of another stupid bitch," As soon as she said it I could tell Kylie regretted it. Kylie had just called Principal Locke a stupid bitch. Oh my God. Oh. My. God. "Excuse me?" "I'm sorry, sounds so harsh. But she has a black eye and she didn't even do anything wrong and you just take Shannon's word for it! Even Shannon's boyfriend said that Emma didn't do anything wrong!" Kylie defends me. I love her.          "McCarthy? Patrick?" She asks. Kylie nods. "I'll call him down. One second," Principal Locke leaves the office and gets her secretary to find Pat's class.Locke wants you.

I text him those three simple words and he sends me a smiley face back, as if that's something positive. As if that's something cute. Five minutes later, Pat's inside and his eyes go big."Oh, wow, the whole crew's in here!" He jokes. Principal Locke shows him to a seat and he sits."What's up Lady Locke?" He asks her. She doesn't smile. I love how Pat tries to act like he doesn't care when clearly he does, as given the impression by his texts. "What happened in the cafeteria?" She asks him pointedly. So he goes through it, clearly defending me, and looking at her dead in the eye. Good."Alright, thanks. You're dismissed. Tell Miriam out there to write you a slip back to class," Pat rolls his eyes. Of course he's not going to take a slip. He doesn't care. He doesn't stand up and instead turns to us.

"Why are you in here?""Because of her," Kylie points to the girl whose name we still don't know."Oh. What happened? Did you get into another fight?" He sounds worried and looks concernedly at me. I shake my head and I nod at Kylie. He smiles and high-fives her. If it were me it'd be a problem, but if it's Kylie it's not. Okay. Interesting.

"Why? What'd she say?" Pat asks Kylie."She was saying shit about my BFF over here so I took the bitch down." Pat smiles up at Zayne, whose cheeks turn red. I don't get it. Are they embarrassed or...? Patrick picks up his bag and Principal Locke says, "McCarthy, you're dismissed. Go back to class or you'll get a cut slip and be sentenced to detention."

Pat smiles and sits back down. "Fine. Detention it is." She writes him a slip for detention after school. Oh my God this keeps getting worse...

Then she turns to Kylie."Miss, um? I didn't catch it.""Fritt," Kylie says through her teeth. Principal Locke nods understandingly. "Hayden's your brother? I can see the resemblance," Kylie nods. She's clearly still pissed off with our principal.

"Zayne, you're free to go back to class," Principal Locke says, before continuing what she wanted to say to Kylie. "Actually, if you don't mind I'd like to stay with my sister," Principal Locke sighs, give a so-be-it look, and turns back to Kylie.

"Four days of detention for you Ms. Fritt. Emma, since McCarthy vouched for you, you're only expected for today and tomorrow, after school detention. And you, Rinna, you've got today and tomorrow as well. I'll checkup later to see who decided to skip. You're all dismissed and Miriam can write you all passes back to class." Everyone stood up at once and exited the office at once. I don't know why Zayne or Patrick would stay when they had the opportunity to leave—it was so awkward and uncomfortable and I still don't know what I'm going to tell my mom. What if this is an omen for the rest of high school? That I'll be spending it in detention? My mom's going to be so disappointed.

# Chapter 13

----------------------------------------

Eighth and ninth period go by rather quickly and next thing I know Kylie and I are making our way towards the detention room. I texted my mom I'll be home for dinner and that I am with Kylie, since I didn't want to tell her by phone what happened. She's going to be so upset. I also texted Zayne and told him to not say a word to mom because I want to tell her. Hopefully he'll be home for dinner though so he can have my back when I give her the news.

Lindsay and Marnie are already seated, in the second row. Kylie and I sit on the opposite side of the room from them. I knew that Kylie attacked the girl—Rinna?—she was called, only because she didn't want me to be alone in a room filled with girls who can't stand me. And I truly appreciate that. I guess that's what best friends are for.

Soon Rinna comes into the room, and then Shannon, and Shannon sits rather close to where Kylie and I are sitting. Shannon is supposed to be a senior like my brother but she got held back when she was in middle school, making her a junior like Patrick. Rinna sits in the far back corner of the room and soon the detention teacher is here. I don't know her at all but Kylie seems to recognize her.

"Cell phones must be placed on my desk and there will be no talking for the remainder of this. Forty minutes of silence. You also need to write a two-page paper explaining why what you did was wrong and how you won't do it again. Anyone who chooses to talk or pass notes or not hand in their phones and are caught, will be receiving an extra day of detention and a meeting with your parents. Be careful," she says before taking a seat and pulling out her own phone. I sigh and take my phone from my purse as well as Kylie's and go to the front of the room and place it on her desk. I go back to my seat and decide to take out the current book that I'm reading, Life of Pi, and divulge in it.

A sign-in sheet goes around the room, three boys show up late and Patrick's still not here. I don't understand how come. Does he not care? After about fifteen minutes, Patrick strolls through the door. His eyes are bloodshot and he has a loopy smile on his face. "Sorry, teach," He says and takes a seat directly next to me. His girlfriend is sitting a few seats behind us and he doesn't choose to sit next to her but instead wants to get me into more trouble.

"Hey babe," he says looking over to me. I tried focusing solely on the book in my hand but I look up to see Patrick with his legs spread and him leaning over with a smirk. "You're hot," The teacher stands up and walks over to Patrick, placing the sign-in sheet on his desk."No talking and hand in your cell phone," she says. He laughs. "Bro, I need my phone though," he tells her. She rolls her eyes. "If you go on your phone then you'll get another day of detention and I'll have to bring in your parents to speak to them. I recommend you hand in your phone." Patrick rolls his eyes and from his desk tosses his phone onto hers. The teacher's eyes widen and she looks irritated."Em why don't you talk to me?""We're not allowed to talk," I tell him. He starts laughing, like really laughing. Lindsay and Marnie are glaring at him and when I turned around to Shannon she kind of looked sad. Not even angry. Just sad.

"Go bother your girlfriend." He didn't even hear me because he's laughing so hard and pretty soon the teacher calls Principal Locke to come on down and take care of him."I'm sorry, I'm so sorry. I couldn't help myself. I mean Emma said that we weren't allowed to talk and I'm just thinking like, bro, this is America. We can do whatever we want! We have freedom!" Principal Locke looks so frustrated with him."I really don't want to have to call your mother, Patrick," she warns. He pretends to take out a key from his pockets, zip his lips and throws it over his shoulder. I can't help but smile a bit. He's so ridiculous. I don't know how he's okay with getting trouble... I must have been gone a while for him to resort to this sort of behavior and him think it's normal.          "Sir yes sir," he tells her before crossing his arms on the desk and putting his head down. Principal Locke and the teacher exchange a few words before she leaves. I go back to reading my book.

After forty minutes of complete silenced hell, with Kylie braiding my hair, we are finally free to leave. Patrick is forced to stay a little after because he came in later, and I hear Shannon tell him that she'll wait for him outside. I leave and as soon as I step foot out the door Shannon grabs my arm and shoves me against the wall. "Listen, friend. I know how much you used to like Pat. And I'm telling you right now, stay away from him. He's mine. You don't want to end up like Lindsay," I look at Lindsay who's coming out the door with Marnie and nod my head. I don't like Pat, so this shouldn't be an issue."Yeah, that's fine. I have a boyfriend anyway," I tell her. She seems to calm down a bit."Okay. Bye, bitch," she says before she turns on her heel and goes next to the detention door to wait for her beloved boyfriend.

I loop my arm through Kylie's and start walking down the hallway. The entire time we are in tears laughing because of how dumb Pat is and how he thinks he's actually funny or smooth or entertaining when clearly, he's not.

# Chapter 14

Dinner went fine. Zayne, his girlfriend Jasmine, me and my parents all ate together. I was content. I told my mom as soon as I walked through the door and she said that she already knew as Principal Locke had called her. She seemed okay though and she said that Zayne told her it wasn't my fault. She was also really concerned about my eye as soon as I walked through the door I could tell she felt bad for me. Luckily it's not like I have any modeling jobs to be at or else this eye would not do us any good.

My parents go over their days as well; my mom went out with Mrs. Wang to the mall and then they had lunch together. She then went to aerobics and came home and made us dinner. Meanwhile my dad was at work up until a half hour ago. Zayne told us that he and Jasmine are planning to go to New York together to look at schools and even, maybe Boston. He also announced some other exciting news: he was offered a full scholarship to Harvard. Of course he was. I'm so proud of my big brother. Jasmine almost squealed because he hadn't told her, he just announced it to all of us as a nice surprise.

"That's incredible sweetheart! Oh my God, I'm so proud of you! Pappy will be so proud. We have to call him. This weekend we'll have everyone over for you, oh my gosh, I'm so proud of my baby," my mom keeps saying. I smile over at Zayne who gives me a knowing look. I'm so proud of my brother also.

Meanwhile my dad clears his throat and tells Zayne that that's excellent news and that he'd be taking the opportunity, right?

"Yeah, Dad. I want to go to their med school anyway, eventually. But I am most likely going to go there and major in physics. So basically our plan is that Jasmine and I are going to fly up there the weekend of her dance recital, which is a Saturday night. But Saturday during the day she is going to look at Julliard or Purchase University and then on Sunday we're going to drive to Massachusetts—Jasmine's uncle lives there and is going to give us a ride, and we are going to check out Harvard and I'll probably miss school on Monday because we want to check out Boston and Lesley University for Jasmine as well," My parents nodded. I don't know how he knows so much about colleges or how to work them. I haven't even thought about it. I don't know how I would deal being so far away from home for years, I feel like that could be hard... then again, you do make other friends. Maybe Kylie and I will go to the same college. Jasmine and Zayne have been dating for probably a year now and they're a cute couple together—Jasmine's extremely art-sy, very involved with school production—I don't really know much about her though because they started dating while I was away but I met her on Easter and she seemed nice. I also saw her on Skype whenever I Skyped Zayne. But that's really it.

"I think I should come with you, sweetie," My mom says to him. Zayne sighs. "Mom, I'm almost an adult. I think I'll be fine." "Sweetheart, this is just such exciting news! I promise I won't intrude on you...or Jasmine, of course. But I'd really appreciate it if I can come. I obviously have to know what's happening at the college and everything. I can book our tickets for Friday night. You and Jasmine can share a room and I'll have my own room, I'll bring Pappy with me too," my mom tells us. My dad seems happy about that. I think Zayne should just let my mom go. I mean, it's good to have an adult who knows what they're doing when picking out a college, right? I loved having my mom with me when I was on the road.

"Yeah, that sounds good. I think it'd be best if you come as well," Jasmine says in such a cheery attitude. "Okay, how about Thanksgiving weekend then? I think we can make arrange-ments," my mom says and whips out her phone, probably look-ing at a very booked calendar. "Mom, Thanksgiving weekend I was supposed to go to Charlotte for a commercial," I tell her. "Oh, right. Well I'll send Kim to take you instead. Don't worry. We'll figure it out." She puts away her phone and continues to eat their meal. My mom looks so proud of my brother. I'm so happy for him. "Plus, we were going to go the weekend of Jasmine's recital which is two weeks after Thanksgiving," Zayne tells her. She nods. Right.

I'm so happy for my brother! I can't wait to tell people that my big brother is going to Harvard. Honestly the Grantz boys are such overachievers. My brother, Keith, goes to law school at Chapel Hill and now Zayne is probably going to go to Harvard. I'm so proud to be their sister!

My sister, on the other hand, is a different case though. I know that my parents don't favor anyone over the other but I guess Kim is just different. She is a smart girl, don't get me wrong, but she's not as intrigued to become a lawyer or a doctor or any of that fancy stuff. She does have her accomplishments though, which is really impressive. I mean, she competed for cheer and won all-states and is also a competitive surfer.

My sister has won so many conferences in surfing from when she was in middle school. Every year she goes to Australia, Hawaii and California for a huge conference. And then she takes part in smaller competitions throughout the year. In high-school she won a lot and my mom always had to take her to these competitions. I think she first started surfing for fun with a few of her friends but later, in high school, she met Lucas who was a competitive surfer and he really got her involved. Two years straight she went to Aruba and Costa Rica. My parents both went with her then—and the whole family went once all together to Aruba and then the second time all together to Costa Rica.

# Chapter 15

------------------------------------------------------------

My sister really is incredible.

Anyway. So I don't know how to go about trying to explain Kim because she's really...unique. She gets bored easily and hates routine. She's a quitter. But she also is daring and always tries new things. When Kim first graduated high school her and Lucas moved to Puerto Rico together, since that's where he was from. I know that Kim took part in a lot of surfing over there as well. She also found yoga there and became a yoga instructor. That's her passion and what she has been doing ever since. Through yoga Kim has been all over the world—even when she came to Paris, she was able to teach a seminar there that was absolutely incredible. I think here in North Carolina she works at three different yoga studios, two full-time and one part-time. She's able to pick when she wants to hold her classes and it really is a fun job. She still is able to surf and that's what she's most passionate about so it works out for her.

Kim and Lucas lived in Puerto Rico together for about a year, until Kim was nineteen and then returned back to North Carolina. Lucas is three years older than Kim so he had already gotten an associate's degree in criminal justice before they had moved and he worked as a surfing coach and as warehouse security on night-duty until Kim graduated high school. Then they took off to Puerto Rico together. I think it was because Lucas' mom got ill and she lived in Puerto Rico and he had grown up with his dad. All I know is that his mom is dead now. I still don't know how my parents exactly felt about it, but I know that my dad was really pissed off that she didn't want to go to college. He called her a spoiled brat and said that he wouldn't leave any of his money to her when he's dead if she keeps acting like that. I thought that was kind of unfair but I can't judge.

Kim and Lucas returned when she was nineteen and he was twenty two. Lucas became a cop and has been ever since, while Kim remains a yoga teacher. So far Lucas has only been able to get two-week' vacation a year, but he also gets a bunch of paid holidays off as well. As time goes on his vacation time gets to be more. They also are probably going to move in together soon since two of the yoga studios Kim teaches at are in Charlotte and that's also where Lucas works. Kim still travels often, even if Lucas can't join her. She'll either go by herself or take Pappy with her or one of her friends to keep her company, depending on what she's going for and how long she is going.

Kim and Lucas really are an inspiring couple; they have been together since freshman year of high school, well, at least since Kim was a freshman. And they've loved each other—even though I know while they were in high school they broke up a lot and Kim did see other guys but they always loved each other. Lucas is basically a part of our family, it's like I have three older brothers not just two. He sticks up for me all the time, he's come on many family vacations with us and he spent some of his vacation time in Paris with my family. I know that at first my parents were against Kim dating him because he hung out with some really bad kids in high school that were known in Hamelton Hills and also because he was older than her, but over time they grew to love him.

Keith walks in through the door while I'm trying to process and compare Zayne andKeith to Kim, interrupting my thoughts. Keith's with his girlfriend, Penny. I don't know much about Penny. I'm pretty sure they've been seeing each other for almost two years now, but he barely comes around with her. Usually he's by himself. Even when they came to Paris together, they were kind of separated from us. At least she was. Oh, and Kim absolutely hates Penny. She thinks that Penny's a whore and a gold-digger, but I don't understand that because I've overheard my mom say that Penny's parents are filthy rich so why would she need to use Keith to get money if she already has money?

"Hey y'all," Keith says as he walks in. My mom bursts the exciting news of Zayne's and Keith congratulates him. Penny even looks excited as well. "Let's all call Kim together and tell her," my mom says. My mom calls, putting Kim on speaker, but there's no answer. She tries calling two more times."Mom, I'm in the middle of a class right now. Why are you calling me?" Kim says in a very frustrated, yet sort-of calm tone. I chuckle. "I have the best news to tell you! Tell your class I say hi! But guess what?! I'm sitting here with your father, Zayne, Jasmine, Keith, Penny and Emma and guess what?! Your baby brother got into Harvard with a full ride! Isn't that incredible!?"

Kim starts squealing on the other end and I hear laughter in the background and she is telling her class about Zayne. "Oh, that's so exciting! Did you tell Lucas? Are you going to go see the school with him?" Kim asks my mom."Yeah, of course we are! Anyway, sweetheart, I'll let you get back to work. We're going to have a little get-together on Sunday for your brother. And remember Saturday night is Emma's Welcome-home party. Are you coming home tonight or staying at Lucas'?" "Probably Lucas'. This class is running late and I still have another one after this and a meeting." My mom lets Kim go and I am just so proud of my family. I love all of them. I love how happy my mom is for us. "I'm going to my room," Keith tells us after he and Penny have gotten food. They go upstairs. Then Zayne and Jasmine go downstairs to the basement. I stay where I am, helping my mom clean up. My dad's sitting at the table with his laptop now, typing. "Honestly, mom, I'm so happy for you," I tell her. She smiles at me and kisses my forehead.

"Why? Because I have the best kids in the world? Even though my daughter manages to get detention on the first day of school..." I know she's kidding and I roll my eyes and help her load the dishwasher. "Yeah, but like... even thinking about Kim, you've done so much for us mom. Like you gave up your job and passion and stuff to help us with our passions. With Keith too, you always were driving him all over North Carolina for football. Kim, forget about it. You did everything for her. You did everything for me. And Zayne you've had to go through so much with him too since he's literally involved in everything. I don't know. It just makes me so glad that you're my mom," my mom has tears in her eyes and hugs me. "I'm so proud of you too, baby," she says to me. I can feel her tears running onto my cheeks. My dad is smiling at us.

"I'm proud of you too dad. I mean. Even this past year, you somehow managed to live without mom. That's how you know that you guys are in love with each other—that it doesn't matter the time, the distance, anything. You always have each other's back.""Your mother and I have gone through everything together. She's my love," my dad says. I sit on my dad's lap and hug him too. "You guys are the best parents. I hope that I can be like you when I get married and stuff," I say to them.

I'm being dead serious—I really do have the best parents ever. They are so strong, they've travelled the world together and they've accomplished their dreams together. I know that they went through really rough times—they got married at eighteen and twenty three, when my dad was first starting law school. They had been together since they were fourteen and nineteen though. They are such a power couple and I really hope one day I can marry someone that's truly my best friend. I hope to think that someone is Peter.

# Chapter 16

I finish helping my mom and go upstairs to my room where I have my laptop and text Peter asking if he's still awake and if we can Skype. Right now he's still in Paris, so that means about six hours ahead, and its eight o'clock here so about 2 am there. He's probably awake. Peter texts me back almost immediately and says of course! So I assume he's probably high or drunk or both and I log onto Skype. I see him face-to-face and am so happy!

"Baby! What happened to your eye?!" he says cheerfully, then worrisome into his mic. I smile at him. "Finally," I say to him. He's playing music in the background."Loren is here, sleeping in my bed. She told me that when I fly back to New York she's going to come also so we can both visit you in North Carolina," I open my mouth, completely shocked and don't know what to say. Loren is a girl I met in Paris—who, for the past three months became my best friend. She's actually from France and grew up there and became a model, she's seventeen, and she's fucking gorgeous. Kylie loved her and we all partied together when Kylie came. I would LOVE for her to come visit me! I met her through Peter so that's why I don't think it's weird that she's sleeping in his bed. More often than not, Loren, Peter and I would all fall asleep together anyway. Yeah, I'm not there, but it's not like he's going to sleep in the same bed as her if I'm not there too. Right now he's laying down on his couch.

"I'm so excited for you to come, baby. I miss you. Do you think you can come for Thanksgiving instead? I don't want to wait until December," Peter processed that in his head and shrugged.

"Honestly, I might be. I have to check. My mom is in Wales right now with my dad and I think we might be in France until December, unless my dad wants to go back to the States for Thanksgiving. I mean, if we aren't doing anything then I don't mind coming by myself. I'll meet lovely Lucas and your sister again," he chuckled. I loved when he was like this—honestly, he does have some sort of accent—a mix of British and French, I guess. It's hard to place because he grew up going to school in New York but he spent so much of his life in France because his mother lived in France when her and his dad met, even though she's originally from Russia. I'm happy though that Lucas made such a good impression on him since Lucas is a permanent fixture in my life and Kim means a lot to me so they have to have a good time together. Lucas is also close in age, twenty four, and Peter's twenty, so they got along pretty well.

"That'd be so great! I miss doing stuff with you. It's been so weird not to...you know," "Roll." He finishes my sentence. I nod. Okay, so when I met Peter it was at an after-party. I was only allowed to go because our personal assistant at the time insisted my mom to let me, which I thanked her for gratefully. We were in England and most of the models I was working with, I'd be working with for all six months and I didn't want to feel excluded so I desperately wanted to go. When I went though, I was shocked. Everyone was on drugs. Literally, everyone. The only sober person there was Peter and that was only because he arrived late. We somehow found each other and he introduced me to ecstasy that night, which is probably my favorite drug. I know it's bad. I know I'm only fifteen. I know I shouldn't be taking ecstasy, but I probably overdid it. After I left England and was in California it was fucking terrible. Like I missed it so badly. I tried massive heaps of drugs, mainly because Peter wanted me to and I wanted to seem cool since I was usually the only American and from North Carolina, not even a popular state where tons of people know—like Florida, New York, California.

I want Peter and Loren here. I love them with all my heart—they're so funny and playful and loud and fun and out-going and crazy. They just do not give a shit. They do what they want, when they want and how they want. Maybe it's because they are bathing in money. Maybe it's because they know they can and they just don't care. Sometimes I just think they were lost on their path, but maybe I'm the same. I don't know how I could end up as a model. It wasn't what I wanted. But I did it. And maybe I'll continue to do it.

"Baby, I'm really tired. I'm gonna sleep. I love you," He tells me. I smile."I love you too. I have to sleep too. I have school tomorrow! Oh guess what? I got detention today. Isn't that great? I hate Pat!" "Pat?" He asks questionably. He doesn't seem jealous. Just curious."Yeah. He's one of my neighbors. He's such an asshole, Peter. He like... loves to torture me. He came high to detention though and like, sat next to me. And his girlfriend was a few rows back and she threatened me. I don't know, long story. That's what happens here in Hamelton!" He laughs."Alright, well don't go getting into too many fights you. Love ya. I can't wait to be there with you, baby," he says to me. I smile at him. I can't wait either."Love you too. Bye!" I sign off and close my laptop, going to my iPod and blasting some Lana del Rey music. I love her songs. I felt so exhausted and so tired and I already had two essays to write, one for Honors English and another for AP History. My history one isn't due until next week though. I get started on my English essay—it's just supposed to be about some book that I haven't even touched upon reading, because I just got back. But oh well. I'll have to sparknotes it I suppose.

# Chapter 17

I'm tired but I don't want to go to bed. I kind of want to text Pat and tell him that I appreciated his antics in detention, but then I wouldn't want to encourage him. I don't really want to talk to him either because I have a boyfriend and he obviously wants to get with me. Which is just a dream for him because I'll never allow that. I do, however slip on the bracelet that Kylie gave me—she said it was from Pat. When I was in Cali he made her take it with her to give to me. I wore it every day since she gave it to me, except on the plane ride. I hate wearing jewelry whenever I fall asleep. I forgot to put it back on my wrist since then though, so for the past few days I haven't worn it but now I feel much more secure putting it on. I don't think he'll notice if I wear it anyway.

I hear Keith and Penny across the hall, they're kind of shouting at each other. At least Penny is—"Keith, I don't want anything to do with your fucking family! They're so fucking up each other's asses and—," "Penny, do not say that. You have no clue the shit my parents have been put through. Nooo idea. They want the best for us, you know that, don't you?""Your mother said that she doesn't want you to marry me! Why? Am I not good enough for her precious son? Am I not good enough for you?" Penny sounds so desperate. I feel kind of bad. And I feel bad that I'm now in the hall, pressing my ear against his door. Keith told my mom about marrying her?"My parents just want me to be sure, Pen. They aren't trying to control me! They just want me to be very sure you're the one, as I'll be with you for the rest of my life. I don't think you should be so offended, your parents are probably think the same about me," I hear Penny scoff and choke out a laugh."My parents love you! They want me to marry you! They think you're the best thing that could've happened to me!""Maybe it's because I put effort in! I truly care about them and they can see that!?" He shouts back angrily. I never heard Keith yell. Ever. In my entire life. He's always the calmest, the sensible, the kind one. Well, at least compared to Kim. The only person he'll usually argue with is Kim and Kim will scream her head off and have such a temper whereas Keith will just sit there and present his points to her like a normal human being. Basically like my mom and dad—my dad will go all lawyer on my mom usually and then my mom will yell about it and then realize my dad's right.

But it's not like Kim and Keith's disputes. Oh no. He actually raised his voice to a yell."Baby, Pen, I love you... I want to be with you the rest of my life. I promise you that. I'm just saying, I don't want to go ahead and do it without my parents' blessing. Just try and imagine how they feel. They spent twenty six years investing their time, their money into me. They literally put all they had into me so that I could have the best future possible and they just want to make sure that I'm in good hands," I hear him say in a calmer tone. She's still quiet. "I don't want to hear about your sappy childhood," she snaps at him. I hear him groan."How can you be so immature about this?! I love you, Pen. You know I do. It is a sappy childhood! My mother was nineteen and pregnant and my dad was still in school and my mom had to work two jobs, gave up her own education for me...she wanted to go to school. She had dreams, Pen. I love you and I love my mom and you shouldn't try to make me choose between the two of you..."

# Chapter 18

"Why? Would you not choose me? Keith, if I'm going to be your wife, you have to understand something. I make decisions in the household. Where we live, how we'd raise our kids. Those are my choices. Not yours. And if you think for a second that I'm going to have your bitchy, judgmental mother apart of our world, you're wrong. I can make you choose, Keith. And I will. She's given me nothing but hell about being with you. She thinks I'm a cheating slut. Why? Because you told her I slept with other people in the beginning, when we weren't even together?! Please, Keith. I don't want to hear your bullshit."

"So you want to... what? Break up with me?" He asks her. He sounds genuine. He sounds hurt. I feel so guilty listening through the door."Are you stupid?! I want you to marry me, Keith. I want us to be married and I want to love you and I want you to not hurt my feelings... I'm your girl, remember? I want us to get married and live in a big beautiful house and have two babies and have a puppy and have Christmas at our house and I want to give you a beautiful home," I put my hand to my mouth to hide my giggle. So she wants to be a housewife. That's nice. If Kim were here, she'd be hating on her so hard... I feel someone tap me on the shoulder and jump, trying not to scream. Zayne is there, Jasmine must have left. He gives me a questioning look so I pull his arm closer to me, so he can listen too. "I know baby. Don't worry. I'll talk to my parents more about it. You know that you're going to have to have Kim in the bridal party, right?"

"Whyyy?" she whines. Zayne looks at me deviously."Because she's my sister. You're having your sister and you have to have both of mine," "Kim hates me and I barely talk to Emma," she says in a baby voice."Maybe you should start talking to Emma and Kim doesn't hate you, relax." What a child. "Emma probably hates me too because of Kim," she says to Keith. She's just making up excuses! "I don't care, you have to have Em and Kim in the bridal party. They'll be so offended if you don't, and you know that. I'm having your cousins in my grooms party so come on, baby. It'll be fine." I hear her groan and then footsteps. Zayne and I crash through the door to Zayne's room, which is directly next to Keith's. We slam the door shut and burst into laughter. "Holy shit," He says to me. I start laughing harder. "I can't believe him. Mom's going to kill him." I know this is true. This is why nobody likes her to begin with!

"I know, I know, Keith's crazy!" "Yeah, he is... Honestly though it's kind of bad that you and mom left because they got so serious. If mom was here maybe she'd have been able to see it more. But it was good that you guys left because Jas slept over almost every night and ya know..." he smiled. I rolled my eyes. I don't need to hear this from my brother, thanks."That's really, really great to hear, bro. I am just... I don't even know. I'm so glad to be home." "Me too. Now you're away from Peter, so that makes me happy. I hear he's a dick." "He's really not! Guys, alright, we have to stop. All of us. We just need to love each other's significant others and get over it. Because Jasmine doesn't make an effort with us, she's really quiet. Penny's a bitch. And apparently Peter's a dick. So this has to stop, let's just appreciate the fact that Jas makes you happy and Peter makes me happy," I tell my brother earnestly. He starts laughing. I love that he didn't try to get defensive. "True, true. And then there's Lucas and he is like our brother already so we can't even say shit about him. If we didn't like him it wouldn't matter because Kim and he are basically married," Zayne says to me. I nod.

# Chapter 19

"Do you mind if I tell you a secret?" He asks me. I look up at him with my eyebrows raised. He hands me a controller, turns his ps4 on and puts in Call of Duty. We begin to play. I'm sort of surprised that I still remember how to play, but whatever. "Alright, so, Jas. She's Muslim. And her parents want her to get married in a few years, they're pretty chill, her whole family. But they all get married around twenty two and her parents had an arranged/suggested marriage so they were talking to us if we want to continue our relationship, I'm going to have to...convert,"

I'm completely flabbergasted. The idea of religion isn't something huge in our household—my parents are Southern Baptist and go to church every Sunday, but they don't exactly make us go also. I mean, I usually do. I like church. But I guess I'm just more spiritual. Kim's kind of in-between religions but very spiritual, I know that Lucas is Catholic and Keith is very, very religious. He's really involved with our church.

"Mom will kill you," I tell him. It's true. He nods. "I don't believe in anything though. I mean, I'm not foolish enough to think that there isn't a God or something divine in our universe, I just don't know what. I don't know. But I don't feel like I'd fit in and that's why I don't know what to do. She told me that there's meetings and stuff I can go to, to at least learn about Islam. If I agree with it, I would definitely do it for her. But I can't get married at twenty two! That's crazy. I need to finish med school, at least, so I'll have some sort of income."

I nod. He's right. My parents always stressed being financially established before getting married since they were in no way, shape or form even close to be financially established when they got married and it really hurt them. "I understand. Anyway, you guys haven't been dating that long to start thinking about it. You're only seventeen, boy.""I love her though." He says it with such finality that I can't help but believe his words. I'm sure he does! I'm not denying that. It's just...how can he be so completely sure that he'd give up what he's thought to be true for the past seventeen years, for a girl that he's not even sure he'll marry? Plus, is he so sure that he'd want to raise his kids like that?  "Well, I support you no matter what you do. If you love someone, then that's it. There's nothing more to it than that." I truly believe what I am saying."Good. You got better at COD since I met you. Did you play with Peter?" I roll my eyes."Yeah, I played with Peter. You're a good brother," I tell him. He smiles at me."You're a good sister."

# Chapter 20

School goes by quick and next thing we all know we're back in detention where the hopelessness is more tangible than ever. Kylie and I sit where we sat yesterday. Pat and Shannon are sitting in the back in one corner, Rinna's in the middle of room, and Lindsay and Marnie are in the front of the room. I want to cry. I just finished the book and now I'm bored out of my mind. Is it a little weird that I got a bit jealous that Pat is sitting in the back of the room? He didn't even say hello to me. Nothing. Maybe Shannon threatened to not have sex with him and that's why he's keeping his distance. Kylie was a little surprised too—he walked past us like we didn't exist. I could tell Lindsay noticed, because she smiled and was happy. Evil bitch. After forty minutes of silenced hell, I walk right out and Kylie follows quietly behind. She knows I'm upset—she knows how I feel about Pat. I feel terrible for being cold to her as she keeps asking me what's wrong but I don't want to talk about it. Not until we're gone. I can hear everyone's footsteps from behind me and they're all sort of quiet, probably trying to listen to what Kylie is saying to me. My phone rings and I don't recognize the number but pick up anyway.

"Hello?"

"Hello?! Is this Emma?!"

"Er...yes," I say awkwardly. Who is this?

"Emma! It's Loren! OMG OMG Peter's been hurt, I don't know what do, Em..." she sounds frantic and crying. I stop walking, my mouth hangs open and I don't know what to say or do. Kylie's looking at me, really worried. She asks if I'm okay. I shake my head no. I can feel everyone from detention's eyes are on me as they begin to slowly pass me by in the hallway.

"Em, I don't know what to do...I called the ambulance, they're on their way...Em, he's so pale, he was throwing up before and he hasn't been responding to me, I just woke up because I heard him throwing up! Oh, God..." Loren's completely panicked. I'm not even in the fucking country with him. I don't know what's happening with him.

"What did he take? Do you remember? Did you guys roll?" I find myself screaming into the phone, tears streaming down out of my black-and-blue eye.

"Yeah, ecstasy, coke. I...we took some heroin," she stammers out through her cries. I want to pass out. How could they do this? Peter promised he's been sober from heroin for the past three years. Why would he do this to himself?

"Holy shit, Lor. Holy shit. Okay...um, um, the ambulance are coming?""Yeah, I can't drive, Em. I kept seeing shit. I did heroin, meth. I...I'm sorry—," I don't want to hear it.

"I love him, Lor, I love him. I can't lose him. Please. Stay with him and make sure he's okay and, I'll stay on the phone with you. Should I fly out back to England? Will it take long, do you think? Is he going to be okay?" I can tell she can barely talk and I know she doesn't have the answer to any of my questions. I see Principal Locke in the lobby when we reach it and I want to die. "Em, the ambulance is here. I'm going to go. I'll call you as soon as I know anything, I love you,""I love him," I say to the dial tone. I sink to the floor with my face in my palms and I start crying hysterically. Kylie's stroking my back.

"Em, what happened?""He OD'd, Ky! He's gonna...what if he dies...Ky, I need to go...back..." They're in France right now but I know that if anything happens, he'll be back in London. Principal Locke is standing before me asking me if I'm okay. I'm shaking uncontrollably—he cannot die! He's the love of my life! "Her boyfriend," Kylie says to Principal Locke. She nods. "I can't...Ky, call mom...please...I need him, he can't die...holy shit he can't die!" I'm screaming this to myself and all I can feel is my shaking and then I feel arms wrapped around me and it's Pat.

He's sitting on the floor with his arms wrapped around me and my tears are falling all over his shirt and staining him and creating puddles and I can't help but wail and cry. Why am

I in America?I feel my phone vibrate and I look down at my phone.The ambulance said it's REALLY REALLY bad, Em. I'm going to be taken in for questioning by police L holy shit... I love you. So does Peter. Remember that. I start crying even harder than I was and I feel like shit and I want to tell her that. I really do. But instead I try to suck up my tears and keep myself calm because I hate making these fucking scenes. I hate it, I hate it, I hate it.Pretty soon my mom's come to the school. She explains herself to Principal Locke on my behalf. Pat makes Shannon leave and my mom takes me, Kylie and Pat home. I'm curled up on Pat's lap, even though he left his car at school. I still have my arms rung around his neck and I can't help but have these incessant gasps of breath. I love him with all my heart. I love Peter.

"Sweetheart, do you think Peter's parents know?" My mom asks me. I shrug. I text Loren asking her, and Loren replies back 'no. nobody knows.' My mom suggests I call his mom and tell her. I can't find the strength to do so though. I don't want to talk to his parents. I want to be there holding his hand. I then dial Anastasia's number and she picks up after one ring. "Hallloo?" She says in her foreign accent into the receiver. I sigh."Hey, it's, um, Emma. Peter's girlfriend," I tell her. "Ah, how are you Emma? You back in America?" "Yeah, I am. I got home on Monday. I was just calling to let you know that Peter...one of our friends called me and told me that he's not looking good," there's a long pause."Eh, what do you mean?" she asks me.

"I don't know exactly. But he went to the hospital. He's still in France, I don't know what happened. She told me that you didn't know so I figure to call you and let you know...""Is he okay?! You mean he's hurt? Is he ill? Or was he physically injured—,""I'm not sure. I can try to find out which hospital he is at for you, but I don't know. I think you should fly over to France though. It seems to be serious."I don't want to seem panicked or frantic or angry or upset or sad, but I know that she needs to get a move on. I know that it is important enough that she should fly over to France. Hell, I'm willing to fly across the Atlantic. "Eh, I'll talk to mi husband. Please, erm, find out the hospital. I'm goin' to make some calls. Thank you for lettin' me know."

"No problem. Keep me updated," I tell her and hang up. I didn't want to say he OD'd. Unfortunately though, now my mom knows that he did and now she knows what kind of guy I hang out with and date. Pat's probably so happy about that. Kylie regretted saying anything as soon as she did it but it's not her fault—I was in hysteria. As soon as I hung up I felt better that his mom knew and I texted Loren asking what hospital he's at. We were all in my living room and I was sitting on Kylie's lap in the recliner seat and Pat was sitting on the couch. My mom brought in chips and dip for us and some orange juice. I'm so grateful to have her as my mom.

# Chapter 21

Hours had passed and Pat was still here. He didn't go back to get his car. Instead, the three of us wound up watching a movie—Uncle Buck—and I anxiously awaited Loren to get back to me. She had texted me once saying he's woken up and is conscious. I was hoping that he would call me and at least let me hear his voice. Pat and Kylie are truly the greatest friends I can ask for. I'm so glad that I have them with me because they just make me feel so much better about myself.

I sat between them, snuggled under a quilt and eating chips. My mom would soon order us all pizza. "I'm going to order two regular pies, one pepperoni, four orders of buffalo wings and two large salads," I hear my mom saying to my dad."Do you think that'll be enough?" "Yeah, more than enough..." My dad says in response. I hear my mom rustling around in the dining room."Well, there's us two...Patrick and Kylie... our four kids, Penny and Lucas and I think Jasmine might be coming by also.

Maybe Hanh and Brance Wang also," my dad mhm's her comments and instead goes back to focusing on whatever he was doing. I hear my mom dial the phone and order. "Guys, pizza will be here in forty minutes," my mom walks into the living room to announce. We all nod. My phone starts to vibrate in my pocket and Kylie feels it also, so she pauses the movie. It's Peter. "Hello?!" I jump up from the couch and run into the kitchen where it's quieter and I'm not surrounded by everyone. "Hey," his voice is hoarse. "Oh my lord, baby, are you okay?" I ask him gently. "Yeah, uh. It's nice to hear you're... your voice," he says. I can hear his breathing and his chest and it doesn't sound great. "I love you...you scared me so much... do you want me to come back?" I ask him.

I'm trying to sound soft and loving and I don't want to seem intrusive or like a clingy girlfriend, especially since he isn't even in the same country as me, but I can't help but be a little worried. I want him to feel loved. "No, I don't think so. My parents are... I'm going to go to a rehab," he finishes. I take a heavy breath. "It's only for a month. I'm going to go to one in Manhattan. I think it'll be... for the best. I'll still be able to see you during Christmastime," he tells me. I smile to myself thinking that's what he knows I'm worried about. "Will we be able to talk while you're there?" I ask tentatively.

"Yes, minimally, I believe. I get a phone call once a week and I'm allowed two days for visitation, but only after my first ten days... they're giving me all the details now. They're making me stay in the hospital another day and then I'm going to fly to New York. I fucked up big time, Emma," I know he did. And at least he knows he did too. I don't know how it could've gone wrong after we had Skyped just last night. He had seemed perfectly fine."Alright, baby. I wish you good luck. I think you should get some rest. Thank you for calling me... I love you. I'll talk to you after school tomorrow, okay?" I ask in a soft tone. "Sure. I love you too," he hangs up the phone. Relief starts to circulate through me and I am so grateful that he's okay and he's not dead. His parents must have been worried sick, especially after they found out it was from drugs. I walk back into the kitchen and I know that everyone is anticipating what Peter had said. "He's okay," I tell them. Kylie lets out a sigh of relief. "Thank God, Em," she says to me. I nod.

"He's going to go to a rehab for the next month... to sort things out. He sounded exhausted so we'll talk more tomorrow." My mom nods. I know she doesn't want me to be hanging around some twenty year old guy. Especially on the fact that he's in rehab now and that he does drugs and of course, she's aware that her precious fifteen year old daughter was brought into the world of drugs because of him. It's not like Keith and Kim weren't smoking pot in their freshman year either, so she shouldn't put so much blame on Peter. I know that Kim has gotten caught multiple times with pot. She was caught by the cops once and by my mom and dad at least a dozen times. Perhaps that's why she wanted to move out so badly. My point is, is that everyone goes through some sort of...experimental stage in their life. Whether it be with their identities or drugs or partying or sex, everyone does it. They want to try new things. Some people take it to a further extreme then what other people do. I personally can vouch that I'm going through that stage right now, without my parents knowledge. Although they probably find it a bit rebellious that I'm with Peter.

# Chapter 22

The food arrives and we all pig out. Everyone's starving. Kim and Lucas just got home, she was at some sort of yogi meeting. Pat and Lucas are talking, hitting it off and I'm eating with Kylie. Kim comes over to join us. Meanwhile, Penny, Keith and Zayne are in deep conversation over some sort of politics. "Baby girls, how are y'all? What happened with Peter? How's your black eye doing?" Kim asks me softly. I shrug.

"It's fine. Peter... he went to the hospital, Kim. He—he overdosed." I stammered out the words as best as I could. I knew that my family probably thought it was shameful—not Kim, but my brothers and parents. Pat.

"Yeah, mom told me he was going to rehab. Are you guys...still together?" she asked curiously. I looked at her incredulously.

"Of course we're still together! I love him!" I didn't realize I was shouting, but now my whole house got quiet and everyone was staring at me. I took a deep breath and Kim rubbed my back."Okay, okay, it was just a question," she says. I roll my eyes.

I've had enough. I throw out the rest of my food—I hadn't eaten so unhealthy since I came back on Easter, and go upstairs to my bedroom. I slam my door shut and I slowly feel all the tears start to stream down my cheeks. I can't help myself. I'm so upset and so heartbroken and it's really unfair.

As I try to catch my breath, I know it's hard and I throw a fist at my bathroom mirror, making it shatter. I should not have chosen to come back to this life. I was doing fine modelling, I was doing fine with my social life, and now... I come back to girls at school hating me, Laura and Melanie barely hang with me, Kylie's had to protect me when she shouldn't need to, a black eye, Peter's in rehab, and Pat's with Shannon. I rather have just stayed far, far away from this place called home. But I know my mom wouldn't have approved if I was alone and I know that she missed my siblings and my father.

There's a knock at the door and I shout "Go away!" before the door begins to open and it's Pat. I wipe my tears away, even though my knuckle is bloody from the glass from the mirror. "What did you—," I shake my head. "Please, just leave," I tell him, trying to hold in my tears from another round of crying. He doesn't budge. He stands there for a moment before jumping into action, first by going to the cabinet and pulling out bandaids for my hand and wetting the toilet paper to clean up the blood. I close my bedroom door so nobody can hear us. Pat sits me down on the bed and begins to clean and we sit in silence. I watch him as he carefully wraps up my hand and then I look at him saying, "Thank you." He smiles at me.

"I want nothing but the best for you, Em," he says softly. I feel his breath so close to my face, it smells of Sprite.

"I don't deserve for you to want anything for me." It's true; I've been nothing but mean to him. I don't want to accept Shannon. I don't want to accept me cutting him off while away. I don't want to accept what happened before I left.

"You were amazing," he tells me.

"What do you mean?"

"Don't tell me you don't remember," he sounds serious. I think he is. I do remember, oh, how I do! He was absolutely incredible. Three weeks before I left...we had sex. I was only fourteen and he was sixteen at the time and he was honestly, incredible. I've never felt a more intense moment then I did with him. After it happened though, we did it quite frequently, for about two weeks, and then the last week before I left I was too busy to see him. I tried not to remember what we had done and to leave it in the past.

"Of course I remember, Pat! Don't you think that when I was in Australia and I had nobody and I was crying myself to sleep from missing you and all I wanted to do was be in your arms—don't you think that I couldn't help but remember?!" He looks down at his feet, before looking back at me and stroking a piece of my hair behind my ear. He looks dreamily into my eyes. "I'm sorry for raising my voice, but—honestly, it doesn't even matter. It was so long ago and well, you have Shannon and I have Peter...so I guess that's the way that it will remain," I tell him gently. He looks so upset and so discouraged.

"I rather you yell at me then not to speak to you at all, Em. I love you. You know I do and you know I always have and you know, you have to know, I always will. Please, let me prove it to you. Blow off Peter and I'll get rid of Shan and just let me prove it to you," my heart basically stopped when he said those three words, those three words that mean so much to me. He's only ever said them to me once, the night before we had sex. And I loved it when he had proclaimed that he loved me. But we were so naïve and so young, and we still are so young. It doesn't really matter. He probably just tells all the girls he loves them so they'll open their legs for him. "I love Peter." I say it with such finality I think it startles him. He looks me in the eyes."No, you don't, Em. I know you don't. Don't say that to me, please," he grabbed my hand, holding it tightly, for a moment the reassurance of him touching me washed through me and I know he's begging at this point and I know these aren't the words that he wants to hear—I know he'd rather have his name coming off my lips than Peter's, but I can't help myself. I don't love Patrick. I never have and I never will. I shake my head, pulling my hand away from his.

"I'll ask Kim if she can give you a ride back to your car." He looks desperate and he's shaking his head. He bites his lip. I can tell there are tears in his eyes. I want to hug him and hold him and tell him it'll be alright but I don't.

"Please," he says in almost a whisper, and suddenly his lips are being smashed on to mine and my eyes go wide, but then they begin to shut and I can just feel the comfort, the stability, the safety, the passion, the excitement, going through my veins so quickly. It lasts a few seconds before I pull away from him and tell him, "You need to go." He gives me a look that's so sad and hurt, even depressed, but I can't have him stay. Peter's going through a rough time and he needs me. I'm his rock. Peter said it himself. Pat leaves my room without saying a word, slamming the door shut. I know that he wants me to be happy and that he wants me to feel better. That's kind and all, but I can't have him. I love Peter. Pat's just a mind game—he always has been, ever since we were kids. All he does is play with girls' feelings, make them love him, and leave. It was the same with me—I played his game and I lost and I walked away. That is, until a couple of weeks before I left for Australia. I got pulled back into it and over time, especially being away and seeing the world for months, I got over it. Pat wasn't my whole world and I don't need him to feel justified or a sense of belonging.

# Chapter 23

------------------------------------------------------------

The next few days go quiet and in passing, school is a routine and suddenly it's Saturday and my Welcome Home Party is today!

Peter and I skyped once since he got to New York, only for a half hour, but I was happy we got to at all. Now he's been admitted into the rehab and I'm happy that he's going to get the help he needs. I might even go up to New York to see him during Thanksgiving break, and again when my mom and Zayne and Jas go up for Jasmine's recital.

Pat's barely looked or talked to me since I denied his kiss. I have to admit, I did feel something. Not love. But something. And I know he felt it too, he probably felt more and I understand that I'm hurting him but he's hurt me so many more times in so many more ways than I have. He was my first;

I know that I wasn't his. And I know he is probably wondering if I had sex with Peter, which I didn't. I couldn't bring myself to do it. Not yet anyway.

My parents and siblings have been doing a lot of work for the party my mom is throwing me tonight. They've all been running around, getting errands done. I was surprised that they all cared so much but I guess that's what I get after being away for a year. They finally care about me.

# Epilogue

-------------------------------------------------------------

**P**erhaps you could think that I don't deserve them to care, I don't know, but I sure am grateful they do.

The Welcome Home party, that I barely deserve, since I completely destroyed my first few days at school and nearly got all my friends in trouble.

I'm nervous though. For tonight. I know Pat's going to show and I don't know how I'm going to deal with him when I'm a nervous wreck and I'm a little bit scared at how he'll act, especially if he is under the influence. Luckily, I'll have my family around me and I'm sure that'll help but nonetheless, I'm still nervous.

"HEYYY!" Kylie comes in like a bat out of hell. She's smiling ear to ear and she has a demonic look on her face.

"How are you, bestie?"

I'm sitting at my vanity, putting on my makeup, even though it just smeared all over my face because of how obnoxious she was.

"I'm actually doing pretty good..." my tone is distant and I know that, but I can't help it because I can't think about anything besides Pat and if he's going to make a scene and god help us, what if he brings Shannon? Are they still together? I don't know.

"I love you, stop thinking so much. We're going to have fun tonight. Think about it: Me and you. Like old times," she threw her head back cackling.

"Are you drinking?" I ask her. She gives me sly eyes and pulls out a flask.

"Take a sip, babe!" she exclaims. I shake my head no, rolling my eyes.

"I'm not going to start drinking so soon! We have a whole night ahead of us. Plus, my parents are right down the hall. I can't step outside smelling like a liquor cabinet," I say as I clean up my makeup from my face.

She waves her hand, taking a sip.

"I'm not going to lie to you but... I'm a little excited about seeing your brother. He's just hot," she says earnestly.

"Kylie!" I yell at her, "You can't talk about my brother that way!" she started giggling and took another sip from her flask.

"Hey, I'm just sayin..." she gets up from my bed and walks out the door, shutting it behind her.

www.ingramcontent.com/pod-product-compliance
Lightning Source LLC
Chambersburg PA
CBHW070452170726
48291CB00005B/1712